Hot Gimmick S

MEGUMI NISHIZAKI

Original Concept by
MIKI AIHARA

Translation by
**Sawaka Kawashima
and John Werry**

VIZ Media
San Francisco

Hatsumi Narita

A second-year student at Takazono High School who lives in company housing. She starts dating Ryoki, but is shocked by a confession from her adopted brother Shinogu. However...!

Shinogu Narita

Hatsumi's adopted older brother and a university student. He has been in love with Hatsumi since he was a child. Unable to bear his feelings, he moves out of the house and into an apartment...

Main Characters

Azusa Odagiri

A classmate of Hatsumi and Subaru's and a popular fashion model.

Ryoki Tachibana

The only son of the most powerful figure in the housing complex. He becomes Hatsumi's boyfriend, but...

Akane Narita

Hatsumi's younger sister and a third-year junior high student. Precocious and good-looking, she is popular with boys.

Asahi Yagi

Subaru's older sister. She has feelings for Shinogu but wishes the best for Hatsumi.

Shuji Kazama

Shinogu's roommate. He and Shinogu always take the same part-time jobs.

Subaru Yagi

Hatsumi's classmate and friend since childhood. He is dating Akane.

Wakana Nanami

Shinogu's friend who is attending the same seminar as he is. She is good-looking and trying to get Shinogu for herself.

Published by
VIZ Media, LLC
295 Bay Street
San Francisco, CA 94133
www.viz.com

Printed in the U.S.A.

First printing, February 2007

Table of Contents

Hot Gimmick S

1 I Fell for Someone I Shouldn't Have

My name is Hatsumi Narita. I'm just an ordinary high school girl like you might see anywhere.

To start off, I'm going to tell you about my crazy days from fall to winter when I was sixteen.

I live with my six-member family in Tokyo's S Ward, at the Higashigaoka company housing complex of the Tobishi Trading Company.

The complex is just like a monarchy. Relations between neighbors strictly follow Tobishi's corporate hierarchy.
In other words, the families of employees with higher corporate positions live in the larger units on the higher floors, and the ladies of those houses are treated with deferential respect by the other women of the complex.

Mrs. Tachibana, the wife of a managing director, is the number one big shot, and she acts just like she's queen.

Allow me to illustrate. If you're taking out the trash in the morning and Mrs. Tachibana notices you breaking one of the rules...you're dead.

Once she came up to me with a pack of flunkies at her heels, and while smartly repositioning her eyeglasses, said, "Isn't your father still a sub-section chief assistant?"

Makes...me...sick!

"Please don't do anything that would tarnish the dignity of our complex," Mrs. Tachibana continued.

Grrrrrr... Patience, patience...

If this is what it's like when you're just taking out the trash, you can imagine how bad things would be in a more serious situation.

It's really frustrating, but I have no choice except to get along as well as possible with Mrs. Tachibana in order for my family to live in peace at the complex.

My grumpy dad is living alone in Osaka on a temporary assignment, but he comes back to Tokyo every now and then.

If someone in our family were to piss off Mrs.

Tachibana, my dad would be "restructured" out of the company, and it's entirely possible our family would end up homeless.

My mom, of course, is the one who cares the most about what the Tachibanas think. She works hard at her part-time job to help make ends meet.

My brother, Shinogu, is two years older than me. He's a freshman at Hitotsubashi University.

Smart? Yeah, and really cool!

Most of the time Shinogu isn't home because his part-time job keeps him busy. He's been my best buddy since we were little, and I'm really proud of him.

I also have a sister, Akane (or Aka-chin). She's a third-year junior high student. Akane is the prettiest girl in the complex. She's popular with all the boys, and if she takes a liking to one of them, there's no holding her back!

She's everything I'm not. Oh, well...

Finally, I have a cute little four-year-old brother, Hikaru, who we call Hii-kun.

He goes to Himawari Kindergarten, which is near the complex.

And then there's me, a second-year student at Takazono High.

I have to take care of Hii-kun—dropping him off at and picking him up from school, among other things—so I don't participate in any after-school activities.

My grades are lower than average at what is sometimes called "Bakazono"—or "Idiot"—High.

On top of all this, my sixteen-year record of having no boyfriend grows longer by the day. Could I *be* any more pitiful? (Please don't answer that.)

One day something happened that threw my family into a crisis. I bumped into *him*.

He is none other than Ryoki Tachibana. Yes, that's right, Mrs. Tachibana's only son.

Ever since he pushed me down the stairs of the complex when I was little, he has been my worst nightmare.

The very thought of him frightens the crap out of me.

Fortunately, after the stairs incident I managed to avoid him because we went to different schools. I was leading a fairly peaceful life until…

…Akane totally freaked me out one day with some major news. "I think I might be preggers," she said. I hated it, but I had to go fetch a pregnancy test for her. I managed to get one, but then, just when I let my guard down, my luck ran out and I bumped into *him* near the elevator.

He was wearing glasses and the white uniform with the blue trim of the prestigious Kaisei Academy. He was tall and his face was…well, not bad, I guess, but his cold, mocking eyes hadn't changed a bit.

I dropped the plastic bag I was carrying, the pregnancy test popped out, and just as I might have expected, he fired off some nasty remark.

Damn, I thought, *I am so dead…*

It would be doomsday for my family if Mrs. Tachibana found out.

In desperation I ran after him…

"Please, I beg you, don't tell your mother about this!"

Forget dignity—I was pleading! But guess what he said?

"Fine. I'll keep quiet, but you have to be my slave."

So that was the beginning of my twisted relationship with Ryoki Tachibana and the beginning of the Narita family crisis.

*

Slave… What did he mean? Well, I found out soon enough!

Without the least delay he measured the size of my

breasts — with his hands!

He called me over to his house, pushed me down on his bed, and said he wanted some *practice*.

He even made me kiss him in public!!

Ooh, the nerve!

Can someone really get away with being so screwed up?

I couldn't take it anymore!

God, pleeeez help me!!

It was then that my prince appeared.

A long time ago, this prince was living in the complex. He moved out of town when we were in the second grade, but then he came back!

My childhood buddy, Azusa Odagiri.

Azusa has grown up to be *gorgeous*, and he has even become a successful model for the popular magazine *Revolver*.

Since elementary school, Azusa had always stood up for me when Ryoki bullied me for not being bright at school.

And he saved me this time, too!

Not only did he save me from Ryoki's evil clutches, but despite all the super hot models at his disposal, he chose me to be his girlfriend! He's just so cute…and *sweet*! He even gave me a cell phone that was exclusively for calls to him! It was like a dream!

Then he asked me out for our first evening date. We went to a trendy club. High on everything, I drank a cocktail and was positively smashed in a matter of seconds.

Fortunately my brother just happened to be working there. He got me a cab and sent me home, but I'd lost my house keys, and while I was pacing around wondering what to do, I stumbled across *him* again. I don't really remember, but I think he went wild groping my breasts.

To make matters worse, the next day he saw an e-mail to me from Azusa saying he'd be waiting for me at his agency's studio.

Pissed, Ryoki followed me there.

But…

Oh…my…God…

Can I really call *this*…my first love?

Azusa never loved me or felt anything remotely close.

He only wanted to get revenge on my dad.

A long time ago his mom and my dad had an affair. As a result, his parents got divorced and his mom died, devastated and brokenhearted.

He only wanted to hurt me, seeing as I was the most precious thing to the man who drove his beloved mother to her grave—that man being my father, Toru Narita. I was only a tool in Azusa's revenge.

Azusa's fellow models had gathered at the studio—or should I say condo?

He had given orders that they could do as they liked with the "prey"—in other words, me—as soon as it arrived, and they all jumped on me like hungry wolves.

Then Ryoki was there, pinning down one of the models and screaming, pressing a ballpoint pen against the guy's cheek.

"Get off her! Or I'll stab you right in the face!"

At this, Azusa's friends froze in fear.

Saved...

...by *Ryoki*...

"Ryoki, do what you want with me," I said in a state of collapse inside the cab on the way home. "I was about to have the same thing done to me by those guys, so what difference does it make?"

Ryoki was leading me to his room when my brother, who had been looking for me, took me home to safety.

Some days later, a rumor spread throughout the complex that Azusa and I had been seen holding each other, and everyone began ignoring my whole family.

This is what happens when you make Mrs. Tachibana mad.

I relied on Ryoki's influence as her only son to help me straighten things out. I don't want to admit it…but I owe him twice now.

Around that time, Shinogu asked me something strange.

"How do you feel about Ryoki? Honestly."

"That's easy. He scares me, what else?"

"You're scared of him? You don't hate him?"

"Why would you ask me something like that?"

He mumbled an answer, but I didn't hear it:

"Because I'm jealous…"

Ryoki started complaining about my worrying over Azusa. Despite what he had done, I thought loneliness might be the actual motivation behind his messed-up actions.

"Don't ever think about any other guy but me! That's an order. You're the one for me. You know what you said before, that I have no feelings? The feelings are there. You're just ignoring them."

When I heard that, my heart throbbed.

Then he took me in his arms...and kissed me...

I'd never felt like that before. My heart had never pounded so hard.

I told Shinogu about that feeling.

He hugged me from behind.

"It seems to me, Hatsumi, that you're falling for him."

"What? As if!"

"I can tell because I love you," Shinogu said.

He was way off. No way would I fall in love with Ryoki!

He slaps, he punches, and he kicks...

He's aggressive, domineering, and self-centered...

And he keeps calling me "stupid" and "idiot."

I don't want to fall in love with him.

I really don't...

*

That same night Shinogu moved out of the complex to live on his own. He's moving to Kunitachi, which is near his university.

He says he's moving because he saved up enough

money from his jobs...

...but why so all of a sudden?

I was shocked.

Then Azusa told me something unbelievable.

"So he finally had to go, huh? Poor guy."

"What do you mean?"

I kept asking until he gave in and answered.

"Maybe he felt like he doesn't belong. In your family, I mean. 'Cause he isn't your parents' kid."

"You're making that up..."

Shinogu...*not* my brother?

I couldn't believe it.

When I consulted Ryoki, this is what he said:

"So what? What's it got to do with me? This pisses me off! I'm going home!"

Then he left me alone in the train on our first date.

But later I found out that he had skipped an important practice exam to be with me that day. I was overjoyed.

He's mean and scary...but sometimes he's kind of nice. I'm not really sure what my feelings are for him.

By chance, Ryoki and I showed up at the same time to see Shinogu at his place in Kunitachi, where Shinogu calmly told us about our dad's affair.

Ryoki got uptight because I was so concerned about Shinogu.

"Why don't you just be all lovey-dovey with big bro' the rest of your life."

He looked...broken.

It was so not him.

Seeing him like that...for some reason I...kissed his hair.

It was the first time I ever...

Then, swayed by emotion...I agreed to be his girlfriend-in-training...

*

Azusa had hired a detective with money he'd earned from modeling, so the truth about the affair between my father and Azusa's mother was undeniable.

My dad—back from Osaka—even got down on his knees and apologized to Azusa.

"You think that's enough? All you can say is you're *sorry*?" Azusa cried.

He stormed out of the shop and I went after him.

"You're impossible to hate," he said.

I was so worried for him. He looked about ready to cry.

"It's funny, though," he said. "After all that, I don't feel any better at all…"

Now that I was Ryoki's girlfriend-in-training, I slowly grew more accepting of him. I even agreed to spend New Year's Eve with him at his family's hotel suite in Izu!

It was our first time, and I wasn't ready for it. When I came back after a little exploration of the suite, Ryoki had fallen asleep on the sofa!

When he woke up in the morning, he blew a fuse because I hadn't woken him up, and then he hightailed it home alone.

I was left behind. Luckily, Shinogu happened to be working at the hotel that night, so he picked me up, and I was able to return to Tokyo.

"Bringing you all the way out here into the sticks and then forcing you to go home alone…I'd call that pretty messed up. Whoever he is, he must not care about you very much," Shinogu said accusingly.

He probably knew it was Ryoki we were dealing with.

Shinogu's right… It's just like he said.

Afterwards Ryoki was awful. He blabbed to everyone —

starting with his mother—that we were going out.

Surprisingly, his strategy worked, and we became officially recognized as a couple by everyone at the complex.

Then, while Ryoki was abroad on vacation, Azusa went missing from home.

When I finally found him, he said he had nowhere to go.

Azusa means a lot to me. Despite what he did, I didn't want to lose someone I had so many memories with.

I took him to Shinogu's apartment...

...where I found a paper with the words "Annulment of Adopted Child Status."

Adopted child...?

Annulment...?

Why would he have something like that?

How *could* he?!

I couldn't believe it...

...and what with one thing after another over the next few days, I was unable to answer Ryoki's long-distance phone calls.

He slapped me across the face as soon as he got back

to the complex.

"I'm not letting you go anywhere with someone who hits girls," Shinogu said, drawing me in close.

But even though Ryoki had hit me, I wasn't scared of him the way I was before.

Mariko-san, the Tachibana's maid, took me to the staircase landing—Ryoki's favorite place...

There he expressed his true feelings for me...

...and I conveyed my feelings for him...

...and we made up.

*

The next test of our relationship was a trap laid by Mrs. Tachibana—who was not at all happy about me dating her son.

She tried to turn Ryoki on to one of the smartest girls at a prestigious high school, an upper-class babe named Ruri Saionji.

Since it would be awful to say in front of him that I didn't want the two of them meeting—even though I really didn't—I said, "Well, since *I'm* Ryoki's girlfriend..."

"Good!"

Apparently Ryoki was pleased.

We went outside and he hugged me. Then I said I was going to drop the "in-training" and be his girlfriend...*for real*.

Around the same time, one of the places where Shinogu was working fell short on hands, so me and my friend Asahi from the complex decided to help out.

Washing dishes at a café...

While I was working there, Shinogu's roommate, Kazama, told me some things that really threw me.

First he told me that Asahi has the hots for Shinogu!

I had no idea...

And there was more.

"Hey, did you know? I've been wondering why your brother's never got a girlfriend. Well, it turns out there's some chick somewhere he's nuts about."

Shinogu in love with someone?

I had never even thought about it.

It bugged me...*a lot*.

Asahi and I secretly followed Shinogu to his next job.

He went inside a bar and was looking at some forms with Azusa. I couldn't hold myself back and confronted him.

"Shinogu! You're always hiding something! Why do

you need to work so much, anyway? Because you want to annul your adoption? Why do you even have that thing? Don't you dare go and submit that form behind my back! It's like you're turning into a stranger…"

Shinogu only replied, "I want to pay your parents back as soon as possible what I owe them for raising me…and then I just want to be *free*."

Then on the way home Asahi hit me with something huge.

"Shinogu's…in love with you, Hatsumi. He's in love with you as a *girl* and he can't stand it anymore… He can't stand being your brother."

Then Ryoki appeared and the conversation was cut short.

I was just sick of it…sick of everything, so I rested my face on Ryoki's chest and cried my heart out.

While in class, Azusa sent an e-mail to my new cell phone.

He told me that he and Shinogu had decided on doing another investigation into his mother's affair. If it turned out that my dad was not the one who had the affair with his mom, then maybe he wouldn't hate me anymore.

I was instantly ecstatic. Then I told Ryoki.

"What a load of crap!" he thundered.

But…he must have already known the truth…

All that time he was just pretending he didn't know anything.

*

Then an "incident" occurred.

Shinogu had come home for the first time in a while, and the two of us got trapped in the elevator.

After half an hour we were freezing.

One snowy day when we were kids we kept each other warm by sleeping next to each other inside some playground equipment until Mom and Dad found us.

Shinogu said he didn't remember…but I knew he did.

We huddled together in the elevator just as we had before and our fingers met and our faces drew close together and softly…lightly…like two feathers brushing… we kissed…

An hour later, after we had been safely rescued from the elevator, Azusa told me Shinogu had loved me as a girl ever since we were kids.

He said I should quit Ryoki and go for Shinogu.

Mrs. Tachibana, who had found out that Shinogu was

actually adopted, showed up at our house one day.

"I cannot countenance my son having relations with a girl from such a family!"

She was in a tizzy, but Shinogu answered coolly.

"I'm dissolving my adoption by the Naritas, so please allow Ryoki and Hatsumi to see each other."

I watched Shinogu walk away after he left the house. He looked so lonely.

Then Ryoki demanded I choose between him and Shinogu.

I stressed over it, and then chose Ryoki. That seemed to make him happy, and the next moment he declared we should run off together!

This time we went by taxi to the suite in Izu.

In the well-lit room of the suite, Ryoki was all over me. I was so embarrassed I accidentally scratched his arm with my fingernails and made him bleed...

He decided to take a shower.

Left alone, I found an old picture inside a side table.

It was of Azusa's mother—and probably Ryoki's father.

Ryoki came out of the shower and saw the picture.

"Azusa's mother's real lover, the one you guys were trying to track down, was my father."

He had heard the truth from Mr. Tachibana a long time ago, and now wore a casual expression as if he didn't care at all.

Having said that, he pushed me onto the bed and resumed.

"You ran away with me. So I'm all you care about now, right?"

Tears gushed from my eyes.

"I can't...can't do this... My family matters to me... I can't forget everything else just to be with you...and I can't be your girlfriend anymore…"

Ryoki forced himself on me all the more, but I fought him off.

"The two of us, it just wasn't going to work."

I fell for someone I shouldn't have.

I tried so hard to make it work.

But I couldn't do it anymore.

It was all just too much.

I couldn't do it...

It was time to give up on it.

I knew it like God himself had told me.

I left the suite alone—to find Shinogu waiting for me.

He had come to take us back to the complex.

"Shinogu..."

It's always you...

...who comes for me when I need the most support.

I explained to Azusa—who was also inside the car—what I had just heard from Ryoki.

That his mother's affair had actually been with Ryoki's father...

That my father was only Mr. Tachibana's fall guy...

And I told *myself* that everything was over between Ryoki and me.

I had made up my mind—even though I hadn't heard what Ryoki said after I left:

"That bitch. If she doesn't want to be mine...then she can just go to hell."

When I got back to the housing complex, I said it out loud.

"I'm never going out with Ryoki Tachibana ever again."

While I was in the depths of despair because of the breakup, Shinogu was kind enough to ask me to go live with him in his apartment.

He never touched me, even when we were all alone.

He cared for me as tenderly as if he were healing a

little injured bird...

"Not right away or anything...but after you've gotten over Ryoki and met other guys and had a lot of boyfriends and broken up with them and stuff..."

He kept his head down.

"After that...if you think that maybe...I might not be so bad after all..."

"..."

"...then do you think you could see me as a *guy*?"

I was told this...by my *brother*.

That's the story of my crazy days from fall to winter when I was sixteen.

If you don't mind...may I continue with what happened next?

2 Shinogu, Take Me and Make Me Yours

The next day at school Subaru told me that Ryoki was home in bed with a fever.

Subaru is my classmate, a childhood friend, and Asahi's younger brother. And surprisingly, he's Aka-chin's boyfriend these days.

So *what* if Ryoki is sick?

It's nothing to me…

We broke up, Ryoki and I.

We come from different worlds, anyway.

He was kind, like, one percent of the time—and the rest of the time he was domineering and selfish. There was no way I could put up with that.

And then there's the problem of Azusa's mother's affair.

My dad was wrangled into a contract with Ryoki's dad to serve as his extramarital decoy. Dad told Shinogu and me everything at the apartment in Kunitachi.

Mom still doesn't know anything about it, or where the money Dad got for the deal came from.

What with that and everything else, Ryoki and I are better off not seeing each other anymore.

If we were to keep on, it would tear my family apart.

So it's better for the peace of my family this way.

So...

...I'm not going to worry about it.

I'm not worried at all.

And I'm definitely not going to go to his...

*

I saw Ryoki and Ruri holding each other in front of his apartment.

"If you do as I say, then I just might let you do it with me..."

He said that, and then he...

After seeing *that* from my position in the shadows, I just had to run away.

I am such a fool.

A complete idiot.

Why on earth did I go there?

"You're the one, Hatsumi."

"No one else will do."

He had said those things to me so many times.

Ryoki…I guess someone else *will* do.

When I got home and opened the door, my brother Shinogu was there.

"Hey, what's the matter?"

He sounded so gentle and worried.

I kicked off my shoes and threw myself into his arms, almost knocking him down.

Then I pressed my lips against his and kissed him.

"Take me, Shinogu. Make me yours."

I couldn't bear the heartache any longer.

"Take me and make me yours, Shinogu. Right now."

If I was with Shinogu, I'd never be hurt again.

I started undressing.

Not only was Ruri good-looking, but she also had a great body.

"My boobs are small…and I'm not even close to sexy, but…"

"That's not true."

Shinogu held me tight, as if to stop me from undressing.

"Take any more off, and I'll explode."

Then he sighed my name into my ears over and over.

"Let's go to my room."

Tenderly, Shinogu led me to his room.

It was best this way.

This way I wouldn't have to worry about anything ever again…

I sat down on his bed, and he gently drew close.

I was looking down, but he lifted my chin.

His face was so sad.

Because I was crying…

He laid me down beneath him and held me. Softly, he kissed my forehead.

Then he slowly pulled back.

"Maybe another time…"

"Shinogu…"

"Just hearing you say that you want to is enough right now."

He took me in his arms and helped me get up.

"You don't have to do this in order to force yourself to forget Ryoki."

"…"

"I'm forcing myself, too. I'm afraid. What if we did this and you got scared of me? What if you hated me afterward?"

"Shinogu…"

"So…I can't do it. Sorry for being such a coward."

The tension suddenly fled my body. I looked up and smiled at Shinogu.

"Thank you…"

I never knew that Shinogu felt fear or doubt.

Knowing he could…I was a little relieved.

But above all, Shinogu didn't do anything because he cares about me more than that.

That feeling…sitting beside each other on the edge of the bed with nothing happening…I was so comfortable and at ease.

I only ever felt that way with Shinogu.

He peered into my face.

"What happened with Ryoki?"

I put my head down.

"Ryoki…didn't care if it was me or someone else…"

"…"

"You know Ruri, right?"

"Yeah…"

"They were holding each other… Ryoki even said that if she does as he says, he'll let her *do it* with him."

Tears began falling from my eyes.

"Maybe you misunderstood. Why don't you ask Ryoki about it?" Shinogu said.

Then he smiled at me in silence.

How could he say something so nice…

I sniffed loudly.

"It's okay. It's really okay. I've already decided to give him up."

That was for sure.

I felt like if I got hurt any more—any more at all—I wouldn't know what to do. I couldn't turn to Shinogu anymore like I had just then either.

"I'm sorry…I'm so sorry, Shinogu."

Shinogu slowly shook his head. Like he was saying, *Don't worry about me.*

Then, without uttering a word, he gently patted me on the head.

Why is he so…

My tears overflowed.

He just kept patting my head.

I was crying because I was sad, but at the same time, I

felt kind of warm and content.

"Shinogu…"

I rested my head on his shoulder.

From the very bottom of my heart, I felt relieved and protected, and was happy…

It really was only with Shinogu that I could ever feel that way.

*

There was a knock at the door.

"Shinogu, I'm coming in."

It was Mom. Shinogu and I quickly stood up.

"Oh, Hatsumi, you're here, too."

She raised her shoulders in surprise.

"Then I came at a good time. I want you to hear this, too, Hatsumi, so come to the living room with us. Your father is here, too."

When we got to the living room, Dad was sitting on the sofa with a stern look on his face. Mom sat beside him.

Shinogu and I sat directly opposite them.

"What about Aka-chin?"

"That girl really vanished fast once her entrance exams were done!" Mom shook her head in disgust. "We'll have to tell her some other time."

She drew in a deep breath and addressed Shinogu and me.

"I think I'm ready to tell you both how Shinogu became our child."

I was nervous and my body was tense.

I looked at Shinogu beside me. He was looking down fearfully.

Mom continued.

"Shinogu might remember, but Hatsumi, you were still small, so you probably don't have any memories of my mother, your grandma, right?"

I nodded.

"She passed away quite early. Her name was Satoko Shinoda and she was a probation officer."

"A probation officer?"

I looked confused, so she explained.

"A probation officer is someone who supervises people who are released from prison, or a juvenile reformatory, to see if they're leading a normal social life. These officers offer help in a number of ways, like counseling people so they can be fully rehabilitated."

I nodded to show I understood.

"There was a seventeen-year-old girl among the people Grandma Satoko was taking care of. Her name was Yuko Tanizaki, and she was a classmate of mine."

Mom's eyes took on a distant look as the memories came to her.

"My name back then was Shihoko Shinoda. Yuko and I were really close. We called each other Shiho-chan and Yu-chan…"

3 We'll Raise This Child as Our Own

"Shiho-chaaaaaaan!"

It was after school. Shihoko turned around when her name was called.

"Yu-chan."

Yuko ran toward Shihoko, her hair floating in the breeze and the skirt of her sailor-style school uniform swishing gracefully about her knees.

Yuko was exceptionally beautiful, and at that moment she looked like someone straight out of a movie.

"Why are you going home so soon? Let's go hang out again somewhere today."

Yuko made a pouty face.

"Hmm," Shihoko said. "But isn't my mom going over to your house today?"

"Is she?"

Yuko put on a wide-eyed expression and tried to look innocent.

Yuko's family, which had moved to town several months ago, was in a bit of a complicated situation.

Her dad had a criminal record for theft, and her mom, for drugs. What's more, Yuko herself was a habitual shoplifter.

Shihoko's mother, who was a probation officer, visited their family once a week to offer counsel and give the family advice on how to carry on with their lives.

"Both Mom and Dad are doing great these days. They don't hit me anymore. And me? I've been a good girl. I haven't stolen anything."

"Hmm, I guess so."

"I'm a model student, right?"

"Yeah…"

"And it's all thanks to you, Shiho-chan."

"What?"

Yuko flashed Shihoko a smile as bright as the sun.

"I mean, no one ever cared about me—only sleazebags who wanted something. Shiho-chan, you're my first real friend. I can tell you anything."

"Yu-chan…"

"When I'm by myself, sometimes I feel so lonely…so lonely I just can't contain myself."

Yuko threw her arms around Shihoko and rocked her roughly from side to side.

"I'm glad I met you, Shiho-chan. I just love you to pieces!"

Yuko didn't care that they were in the middle of the street. She kept repeating how much she loved Shihoko.

"Okay, I got it!" Shihoko said, laughing. "I love you, too, Yu-chan!"

"Really?"

Shihoko answered with a big nod and finally freed herself from Yuko's embrace.

"But go home today. You want to show my mom how great you're doing, don't you?"

Yuko was looking at Shihoko and pouting.

"Okay."

And with that, she began lazily walking down the side street leading to her house.

＊

Shihoko hurried along the way she had been going.

She was going to be late.

She rushed along and turned left. A small park came into view.

"Shionoya-kun...I wonder if he's already there..."

She had met Satoru Shionoya in the student council.

They had fallen into the habit of going home together after the meetings, stopping to chat in the park.

The other day he had gently held Shihoko's hand and told her he liked her.

He was Shihoko's first love.

Student council was held only once every two weeks.

They couldn't wait that long to see each other, so they had chosen the day of Yuko's probation observation for their next meeting.

Shihoko's heart pounded madly from the short run—and her nerves.

"I'm sorry! Did you wait long?"

Satoru raised his head from the paperback he was reading.

His fine-featured, intellectual face befitted him as president of the student council.

"No, not much. Sit down and catch your breath."

He smiled pleasantly.

"I got caught up with a friend."

Shihoko had sat down on the bench and was wiping the sweat from her forehead with a handkerchief when…

"Oh, it's Shiho-chan!"

Yuko appeared out of nowhere.

"Yu…Yu-chan…"

Yuko should have already been home.

She must have followed Shihoko after they parted ways. Yuko was good at sports, so her skin was perfect, without a drop of sweat.

"Am I getting in the way?"

Shihoko bit her lip.

"Not at all. Don't just stand there, come sit with us."

Yu-chan responded to Satoru's invitation with a brilliant smile.

"Is it really okay? I'll join you, then."

She sat down beside Satoru—not Shihoko.

"You're Shionoya-senpai, right? The student council president."

"How did you know?"

"Well, you're smart and good-looking…and famous for being just about perfect."

"You're just teasing me. If I'm not wrong, you just recently transferred in, right? And I see you're friends with Shinoda-san."

"That's right. Really close. No secrets between us."

"That's great you've got a best friend. I'm envious."

"You don't have one, Senpai?"

"Well, let's see...a best friend..."

He couldn't peel his eyes off her.

"Oh, by the way, what's your name?"

"Mine? Yuko Tanizaki...that's me!"

"So...Yuko-chan, then."

Shihoko could only sit and listen in a daze.

Time flew by and night fell, so they decided to go home.

Yuko and Satoru were going in the same direction, so they walked home side by side.

*

The next morning Yuko came up next to Shihoko on their way to school.

"That's what you get for keeping secrets."

"..."

"I trusted you...and now my bad habits are back."

"Don't say that…"

Shihoko looked at Yuko with puffy eyes from not getting a wink of sleep the night before.

"That's because if I'd told you…"

"You were worried I'd steal your boyfriend."

Shihoko looked down.

"You didn't trust me at all!"

Yuko stormed past.

"You're wrong! It's because guys find you so attractive…"

Yuko turned around.

Against the sun, it looked as if she were glaring hatefully at Shihoko.

Finally, she spoke.

"You were just feeling sorry for me 'cause you're the daughter of the probation officer."

Yuko stopped coming to school the next day.

And Satoru evaded Shihoko's eyes whenever they met at school.

According to Shihoko's mother, Yuko was spending her days listlessly at home and her nights going out with her boyfriend.

"All she does is brag about her boyfriend. Shihoko, do

you know him?"

"No."

"Why don't you go visit her? You two were best friends."

"Yeah…"

But Shihoko never made that visit.

Then she heard rumors that Satoru had started skipping school, and that he had been removed as student council president and his grades were plummeting.

Several months after the day the three of them had met in the park, Yuko and Satoru disappeared, as if they had eloped.

Even then a new life was growing within Yuko's body.

*

Five years passed.

Shihoko graduated from a local junior college and entered into an arranged marriage with a man named Toru Narita who worked for a trading house. She became the mother of a little girl named Hatsumi, now two years old.

"Hatsumi finally fell asleep."

Shihoko had come back to her familial home with her little girl for the first time in a long while. She sat down beside her mother, Satoko.

Satoko had lost her husband two years before, and all of her children were already out of the house, so she was living alone.

Maybe it was because they lived near each other that her youngest daughter visited the most often.

"Well then, let's relax and have some tea."

Satoko went toward the kitchen.

Then the doorbell rang. *Ding dong*.

"I'll get it."

Shihoko stood up, undid the chain, and opened the door.

A woman and a skinny boy of about four were standing there.

The woman—the boy's mother?—was even skinnier than he was.

"Shiho-chan…is it you?"

Shihoko hadn't realized who it was until she heard the voice.

"Yu-chan! Can it really be you? Yu-chan?"

"Yes, yes…"

Tears began rolling down Yuko's cheeks.

The radiant beauty she had possessed five years ago

had completely disappeared.

Her complexion was dark, her eyes were dull, and she even had some white hair.

"Look what has become of me…"

Shihoko and Satoko let the pair come inside and decided first and foremost to listen to what Yuko had to say.

"Where's Shionoya-kun?" Shihoko asked. Over the years, her resentment had all but disappeared.

"He left us about two years ago. At first he was working hard, but then he said he wanted to go to university…he said this wasn't his life…"

"So you raised the child on your own?" Satoko asked.

"Yes," Yuko answered. "There was this cocktail bar that would look after him in back while I…"

Yuko said she had met some guy at the bar. He worked at a small factory and they were living together.

"What's your name, little boy?" Shihoko asked.

The boy kept his mouth clamped shut and would only look down.

Maybe he was nervous. He didn't move at all.

"His name is Shinogu," Yuko answered for him.

"Shinogu-chan, huh? That's a good name. Here, have some candy. It tastes really good."

Satoko gave the boy a piece of candy.

As she did so, Satoko was startled by something she glimpsed beneath the boy's ratty T-shirt.

"Excuse me."

Satoko firmly made the child take off his shirt.

When the truth became apparent, Shihoko put her hand over her mouth in shock.

The boy's body was covered in horrible scars and bruises.

"Is the man who lives with you responsible for this?"

Satoko gazed at Yuko with piercing eyes.

"When he loses at gambling...he..."

Shihoko, with tears in her eyes, helped the boy put his shirt back on.

"And you. You're an alcoholic."

Yuko reacted to Satoko's comment by looking down.

"If that were not the case, the Yu-chan I knew would have never come to look like this."

Yuko started moaning as if in pain.

"And you hit him, too, don't you?"

Crying, Yuko nodded deeply.

"I didn't know what to do... It seems my parents got

divorced, but nobody knows where they are... Then I remembered you and how much you had helped us so long ago..."

Yuko was weeping bitterly, her head on the tatami floor. Satoko and Shihoko looked into each other's eyes.

*

"Stop. Don't hit me!"

At the sound of the boy's voice, Shihoko rushed into the apartment.

"Don't do anything unless I tell you to!"

Yuko was mercilessly striking her son in the face.

"What are you doing?"

Shihoko went into the room and snatched Shinogu away from his mother.

The poor boy. Not only his body, but now his face, too, was swollen.

"How awful..."

"The little brat tried to hide the saké bottle..."

Yuko tried to hit Shinogu again, but Shihoko embraced him tightly in protection.

Since Yuko had appeared at Satoko's house, Shihoko and her mother had been taking turns visiting her.

Whenever they brought sweets or other food to her, Yuko would bow her head to the tatami floor and thank them over and over again.

Every single time, she promised to stop beating the boy, to stop drinking, to leave the man she was living with...

This went on for about half a year.

Instead of pulling herself together, however, Yuko just got worse and worse.

"Hey, you're workin' the bar tonight, aren't ya?"

Shihoko's body froze when she heard the man's voice.

He lay in the corner of a grungy room reading a horseracing newspaper.

This was the first time she had seen the man—who had stopped working a long time ago and was always out gambling.

Maybe he didn't have any money to gamble with anymore.

He stood up and glowered at Shihoko.

"I want you to knock off all the favors. Because of you, the kid is even less tolerable than before."

He tore Shinogu from Shihoko's arms and kicked him

in the stomach.

The impact knocked the boy all the way back to the wall and into a sliding screen.

"Stop it!"

Shihoko threw herself past the boy's mother, who was just standing there stunned, and rushed toward Shinogu.

"Are you okay? That must have hurt. Are you all right?"

Shinogu's face was distorted in pain, but he didn't say a word.

She hugged him and felt him ever so slightly hug her back.

Shihoko's heart flared with anger.

"Do anything so cruel again, and I'll turn you in for child abuse!"

As if not hearing Shihoko at all, the man began yelling at Yuko.

"You be sure to get an advance on your salary tonight! You got that?"

Kicking the clutter out of his way, he left the room.

"Where's he going? There isn't any money, right?" Shihoko asked Yuko.

"If he's here, the debt collectors will come…"

"Debt… Is it big?"

"One point five million yen…"

"…"

"Before we knew it, it had gotten out of control…"

Yuko started pouring alcohol down her throat from a bottle of saké she had just found.

"Stop it! You said you were going to stop."

Shihoko tried to take the bottle, but Yuko snatched it back with surprising strength.

"If I don't have this, I can't move. I get frustrated and can't do anything. This feeling…this way of living…you would never understand! You don't know what those debt collectors can do to you!"

She downed the rest of the bottle.

"Yu-chan! Don't! Try harder. You have to get better. You have Shinogu to think about. Don't you feel sorry about what this does to him?"

Yuko covered her face with her hands.

"Shinogu…"

She burst into tears that wet her whole face.

"Let's work on it together. Stop drinking, break up with that good-for-nothing man of yours, and start a new life with Shinogu!"

Shihoko shook Yuko by her bony shoulders.

"Shiho-chan…you're so kind…even after the terrible

thing I did to you."

"What are you talking about? That was a long time ago."

"I'm being punished for what I did to you when you were such a good friend to me."

"Yu-chan…"

Yuko smiled through her tears, then collapsed to the floor.

"Yu-chan?"

Shihoko shook her, but Yuko lay limp. No response at all.

"Yu-chan! Yu-chan! What happened?"

Something was wrong.

"Yu-chan, hang on!"

First of all, she needed to call an ambulance.

Shihoko grabbed the phone and dialed 911.

But the call didn't go through. The phone service had been stopped.

"Shinogu-chan. Look after your mother."

The boy nodded firmly.

Shihoko saw he would, then ran to use the neighbor's phone.

*

After simple treatment at the hospital, Yuko was transferred to a specialized institution.

However, she had lost the will to keep living.

She refused to eat, wouldn't speak a word, and without anyone at her bedside, passed away a week later.

She was only twenty-three years old.

While Yuko was in the hospital, Satoko looked after Shinogu.

When the man Yuko had been living with didn't show up at the hospital or the funeral, Satoko left a note at his apartment saying she would be taking care of Shinogu from then on.

Shihoko was temporarily relieved.

This way, Shinogu would not have to live in terror.

Shihoko crouched down and put her hands on Shinogu's shoulders.

"Live your life to the fullest for your mom's sake...for Yu-chan."

The very next day something happened.

"Mom?!"

Shihoko couldn't believe her ears when the hospital phoned.

Satoko had collapsed from a cerebral hemorrhage. She was taken to the hospital but died soon after arrival.

"Mom…"

Rubbing her mother's already cold hands in her own, Shihoko wept.

"You must have been tired…from taking care of Yu-chan…and everything else."

"It seems it was the boy who called the ambulance."

A relative pointed at Shinogu.

The boy must have remembered everything Shihoko had done when his mother had fallen ill.

"What a good little boy," someone else said. "Just amazing. Whose is he?"

"Oh, an acquaintance's."

Shihoko managed an ambiguous reply for the moment.

The funeral ended without incident and only relatives remained afterward.

Shihoko's mother had left a will, and there were no problems whatsoever in handling the inheritance.

Shihoko raised her voice when everyone looked about ready to leave.

"Actually, I need to talk to you about this boy..."

Then she related the story of Yuko's tragic life and looked around at her relatives.

"Is there anyone who can take him in?"

"We hear what you're saying, but...we don't have the extra money or space."

"With three kids, it's already hard."

"We don't have any kids, but my husband just hates children."

"It's too late for me to raise any children at my age."

"Why not hand him over to an orphanage?"

Shihoko shook her head.

"This boy needs affection. A family's warm affection."

"Then why don't you take care of him, Shihoko?"

Without saying anything, Shihoko put her hands over her stomach.

"Oh, you're already going to have your second."

The conversation had reached a deadlock.

"Well then...doesn't it make the most sense to return him to the girl's common-law husband?"

"No! If we do that..."

Shihoko was about to stand up...

...but froze when she saw the man who had just slipped into the room.

Shinogu had been waiting in the next room. Shihoko brought him to her and clutched the boy to her chest as if to show how much she did not want him taken away.

"What...what did you come here for?"

"Wow, so the old bag finally bit it, huh? That's what you get for going into someone else's house and meddling in their business."

The man's gaze passed over the faces of the relatives.

"What are you all looking at? I came to pick up Shinogu—of course!"

"You didn't even come to Yuko's funeral!"

"That woman was useless. Useless!"

He cast a glance at Shinogu.

"But her brat may yet turn out to be of some value. He's got mettle, and brains to go with it..."

"So what? I'll never give him to you."

"Then who's gonna take care of him?" the man said.

At this the room became so quiet you could have heard a pin drop.

Raising any child not one's own would be difficult, but who would want to raise a child that a creep like this was after?

"Huh? Who's gonna do it?"

He stamped a foot in irritation.

"I...I will. I'll take care of Shinogu," Shihoko said. "We'll raise him as our own."

She knew that her husband Toru, sitting beside her, was staring at her in disbelief.

A murmur passed around the room.

"Shiho-chan, do you know what you're saying?"

"I wonder if she can handle it?"

The man crouched down by Shihoko and whispered into her ear.

"I'll let you, if you take the debt as well."

"..."

"If you don't..."

The man ran a finger lightly down Shinogu's cheek.

The boy's whole body went completely still—as if he was petrified with fear.

"Okay...we'll take that, too..."

Shihoko's voice was trembling.

"That's great to hear."

The man stood up.

After a cursory look at Shihoko, he swaggered out of the house.

*

Shihoko and her husband took Shinogu, who was still recovering from the bruises he received from his mother and her man, back home.

Shihoko spoke to the boy as he was sitting holding his knees in a corner of the room.

"Shinogu-chan. You don't have to worry about anything anymore."

"..."

"From today on this is your home. We'll all live here together."

A neighbor had looked after Hatsumi, who had a slight fever, during the funeral. After Shihoko had picked her up, she introduced her daughter to Shinogu.

"Hatsu-chan. This is Shinogu-kun."

"Shinogu-kun?"

Hatsumi tilted her head to one side.

"Yes. Starting today, he's your brother."

Hatsumi's eyes brightened with delight.

"Brudder? Hami-tan want brudder."

Hatsumi moved toward Shinogu.

"Brudder, brudder."

Shinogu hid himself behind Shihoko.

"Why hiding?"

"Your brother is a little shy," Shihoko said and smiled.

She thought that despite all the difficulties that lay ahead, the smiles of the children would save her every single time.

But first and foremost, she had to bring back Shinogu's smile. She swore to herself she would.

That night Shihoko and Toru faced each other across the table.

"I am so sorry. To make the decision myself like that…"

Shihoko apologized to her husband with her head hung low.

"How in the world did something like this happen?"

Shihoko hadn't told Toru much about how she had been taking care of Yuko and Shinogu.

"I didn't want to worry you."

"Hmmm…" Toru growled sourly. "And it turns out Shinogu is the child of your first love."

"Yes, but anyone who'd seen what I had would have wanted to do something."

"There's a limit to being kind! We're going to have another baby, you know."

"I'm so sorry."

"You don't have to apologize anymore."

"But there's one more thing I need to apologize for."

Then Shihoko muttered that she had also taken up Yuko's 1.5-million-yen debt.

"What?"

So that's what that man whispered in your ear, Toru thought, biting his lip.

"So what are we going to do about that?"

"I'm thinking about paying it with the inheritance from my mother," Shihoko said. "I think Mom would be happy if it meant saving Shinogu-chan."

"Hmmmm…"

"Please. Think of him as our own…and take good care of him… After the baby is born, I'll work part-time to help make ends meet."

At first Toru was silent.

Eventually he said, "I'm not going to go out of my way for him."

Shihoko smiled.

"You're…you're already doing more than enough, Toru…"

Shihoko went to the children's room. Shinogu was sleeping like the dead. He must have been through countless sleepless nights by now. Hatsumi, asleep beside him, was mumbling in her sleep.

"Brudder. Let's pway, Brudder."

Shihoko thought how great it would be if her daughter Hatsumi, always friendly, could revive Shinogu's spirits.

"Help me out, Hatsumi. Okay?"

Shihoko softly ran her hands through her three-year-old daughter's bangs.

4 You're Not Alone

Mom drew in another deep breath.

"And that's the end of the story."

I nodded, trembling.

I had never imagined that Shinogu had such a past...

When he came to our house I was only three years old, so I just took it naturally that I had a new brother.

I didn't have the slightest idea why he was now taking on so many different part-time jobs.

I was so clueless...and was always saying Shinogu this and Shinogu that and relying on him.

"Shinogu," Mom said.

Shinogu raised his head slightly.

"I didn't take you because I had to. I took you because I *cared* about you."

"Mom…"

"I'm so happy that you grew up to be such a great young man. You're so tender and caring toward your sisters, and—even though it doesn't come from us—you're intelligent and good-looking, too! Really, Shinogu, you are the Narita family's pride and joy."

Shinogu lowered his head again, as if nodding.

"You wanted to go to medical school but gave up because of the money, but for you, your father and I would have done whatever it took to come up with it."

Dad, who had been quiet all this time, finally opened his mouth.

"It's just as your mom says. When you had just arrived, I couldn't forgive your mother for making a decision like that without consulting me. If I unconsciously treated you coldly, I have to apologize for that…"

Shinogu shook his head emphatically.

"I never noticed anything like that."

That's understandable.

Shinogu was always being hit and abused until he came into our home.

"Now, you may do as you wish, Shinogu. We'll stand beside you whatever decision you make. You can make your own choice."

When it came to the annulment of adoption...

I think Shinogu had already made his decision.

To be free?

Or because of his internal suffering? Because of...
me.

"I was five years old, so I do remember a little...but I'm really happy you told me all this. And while I don't know how to say it very well, thank you for everything..."

Shinogu was looking down and speaking softly.

His bangs were covering half of his face, so I couldn't see his expression.

But I think he was crying...

Fighting back my own tears, I took Shinogu's hand, which was atop the sofa, and held it tightly so our parents wouldn't see.

Shinogu turned almost imperceptibly toward me.

His eyes, now barely visible through his hair, were wet, as I had expected.

And his hands were trembling.

Shinogu.

Have all those bruises you got when you were little really healed?

It must have been so hard.

It must have been so lonely...

But you're not alone anymore.

We're here for you, and even if you annul your adoption...I can't say it well, but I'm always on your side and I'll always be there for you.

Shinogu smiled slightly, as if he knew what I was thinking.

5   If Your Happiness Runs Out,
       I'll Give You Mine

Shinogu left the house early the next morning. He said he had to work, so he was going back to Kunitachi.

"I'm leaving too!"

I was slipping on my shoes as fast as I could when my mom yelled for me.

"Going to school so early? Can you take out the trash?"

"Not today. I gotta go."

The door slammed shut behind me and I drew a deep breath.

As if I had time to take out the trash!

I'd probably end up having Mrs. Tachibana tell me something like, "After all, compatibility is a matter of being equals."

Anyway, I started following Shinogu.

When he got to the station, he went to the platform for trains heading away from Kunitachi.

"I knew it…"

He changed trains twice before getting off at a small station. I shadowed his every move as skillfully as a professional detective.

After a short walk, he stopped in front of a building. It looked abandoned. No more than ruins, really. Half of the doorplate—which bore the name we had heard from Mom yesterday—had been chipped off.

From behind, Shinogu looked lonely as he stood in front of what was once an institution for alcoholics.

I watched him from my hiding place behind a nearby telephone pole. In my heart, though, I wanted to run out and throw my arms around him.

"Shinogu…"

It was an almost inaudible whisper, but…

"It's about time you came out from there."

I jumped in surprise, then I slowly walked over beside him.

"Uh…how long have you known I was following you?"

"Since right after we left home."

"Erg…"

"Hatsumi, you'd never make a good detective."

"…"

*

Shinogu and I looked up at the dilapidated structure.

"It's a bit sad, isn't it?"

"Yeah…"

"Shinogu, you're not thinking about looking for your biological father, are you?" I asked, afraid of how he might answer.

Shinogu's biological father was Satoru Shionoya, Mom's first love.

He'd been president of the student council. That's why Shinogu's so smart.

No wonder my brother is so different from me and Aka-chin!

His dad is probably someone important by now.

Shinogu shook his head in response to my question.

"No, I don't want to meet him."

Was I ever relieved to hear that!

If Shinogu found his real dad, he might choose to become a member of that family rather than ours…

"To tell the truth, it's not like I would want to see my mother either, even if I could. I was always so scared of her, and she was always so angry at me. That's the only image I have of her."

"But isn't that why you came here? Because you wish you could see her?"

Shinogu shook his head.

"She was here. She died here. I just wanted to make sure of that. That's all. It's strange, but that's all I wanted."

"..."

"It's funny, isn't it? I guess I'd be lying if I said I didn't want to meet her, but the truth is, when I try to picture my mother, I only see the face of our mom. The same goes for Dad. Thankfully, this opportunity arose to make me realize that I am Shinogu Narita..."

"Shinogu..."

Shinogu—usually quiet—was being really talkative, maybe to help him organize his thoughts.

"I...when I first started settling into life with the Naritas, even though I was only a child, I thought, at least I'm not being hit every day for God knows what...and, quite the opposite, you and Mom both cared for me so much, calling me 'big brother' and 'son'...and Dad, while he's never easy to read, watched out for me silently but affectionately. I thought maybe I was learning what it meant to be happy."

Shinogu paused for a breath.

"Then one day I was overcome by fear. You know how there's a limit to how many chocolates and sweets you can have? Like that...I thought, what if there is also a limit to the amount of happiness you can have? If I'm this happy now, maybe it's all going to run out soon. I can't let that happen. I should be careful how much happiness I use up. If I don't, it'll run out. I was worrying about that all the time."

"Shinogu..."

I was so used to the happy life I was leading that I'd never thought about it.

But Shinogu, who had experienced some of the worst the world has to offer, thought about things like that.

"Even now, the fact that you're here...together with me...makes me so happy. Maybe my lifetime's worth of happiness is about to run out."

Shinogu shrugged his shoulders wryly.

"That won't happen," I said.

I couldn't stand to hear him talk that way.

"If your happiness runs out, I'll give you mine."

"Hatsumi..."

"There's bound to be more if we put our happiness together, and if that's not enough, we can work hard to make more. I'll make more happiness and put it in your pocket. And just so it'll never run out, I'll always add more…whole gobs!"

Shinogu's eyes were fixed on me.

He was clenching his fists inside his coat pockets as if trying to hold something back…

I stared at him anxiously.

Had I just made a confession of love? What would I do if he took it that way?

I hadn't meant it to sound that way. I had just wanted to cheer him up because he was saying such sad things.

Shinogu smiled as if to tell me he understood.

"Hatsumi, you're the sweetest."

Shinogu patted my head gently.

"Hey, if you don't hurry up, you'll be late for school."

"Oh…you're right. I'll probably miss my first class. Dammit!"

"Shall we go, then?"

Shinogu spun around, putting the building behind him.

His spirits seemed brighter than I had seen for quite some time.

I thought it would be great if he had finally found some closure.

We took off in a jog for the station.

Shinogu.

You've become more of a Narita than ever, haven't you?

So never leave me.

Don't annul your adoption...

...whatever your reasons.

Please...don't do it.

I repeated these words softly within my heart again and again.

6   We Just Missed Each Other

Spring break.

When I took out the trash one morning, all the housewives had formed a circle and were deep in conversation.

"Did something…happen?"

"Oh, well if it isn't Hatsumi Narita!"

They pulled me into their circle.

"The Tachibanas are leaving the complex."

"What?"

"You're Ryoki's girlfriend, aren't you? Tell us why they're leaving."

Startled, all I could do was stammer.

"Uh, well…me and Ryoki…we aren't dating anymore…"

"*Really?!*"

They closed in on all sides.

"Urgh! Excuse me. I need to go now."

I scurried out of the circle and somehow got away.

Ryoki…is leaving…

He's leaving…

My legs unconsciously led me to that place—the landing at the top of the emergency stairs.

Ryoki's secret base.

The metal stairs clanged under my feet.

I went up slowly.

But Ryoki wasn't there.

The landing was where Ryoki and I began, where he pushed me down the stairs when we were kids.

When I was his slave…and then his girlfriend-in-training, I could always find him there.

A lonely wind was blowing across the landing now that its master was absent.

If Ryoki had been there, what would we have done?

But I guess we just missed each other.

Nothing could be truer.

*

Later that day, Akane burst into my room brimming with excitement.

"You went out with Subaru today, didn't you? What happened?" I asked.

"Hatsumi, before we get to that, I've got some hot news for you. I came back from my date early because I wanted to tell you so bad!"

Aka-chin plopped down in front of me and opened her mouth.

"Mr. and Mrs. Tachibana have decided on a separation that will eventually lead to a divorce."

"Huh?"

"You wanna know why?"

"Y-yes."

Aka-chin scooted closer.

"Because it came out that Mr. Tachibana once had an affair!"

Omigod...

"Aka-chin, where did you hear this?"

"Subaru heard it all from Ryoki. But there's more. Who do you think was his mistress? Huh? Huh?"

"..."

"Now don't be surprised. It was Azusa's dead mom!"

It would have been better, Aka-chin, if you had never found out…

Apparently Ryoki had spilled the whole story to both his parents.

I can just imagine the look on Mrs. Tachibana's face when she heard.

According to Aka-chin, Ryoki's father wasn't surprised at all. Rather, he owned up to his love for Azusa's mom, and then refused to apologize.

"But it majorly irks me that Dad was used as the fall guy all this time."

Aka-chin snorted angrily.

I thought a minute, and then put it to her flat.

"Akane, you can't say a word about this to Mom."

"I know, I know…"

She pressed her lips together, and then went on.

"And do you wanna know about Ryoki?"

She looked at me searchingly.

"No…not really."

"You sure? Really sure? Really, really sure?"

"Ok…um…I'll listen. Just in case," I said faintly.

Aka-chin beamed.

"Now…who do you think Ryoki will go live with, his

father or his mother?"

That father.

That mother.

I couldn't imagine Ryoki choosing either one.

The Tachibanas, although they look like a family, aren't really a family at all. That's why Ryoki could never understand why I care about my family the way I do.

"I don't know."

Seeing me give up, Aka-chin rattled off the answer.

"He's going to live in the school dormitory. Right now he's staying in a hotel and being taken care of by his maid, Mariko-san."

No matter what happens, there's always someone there for Ryoki.

He's never completely alone. Not like Shinogu. Not ever.

But Mariko-san told me something once.

"Please, always be there for Ryoki-sama," she said. "Be there for him, because he has always been alone."

I think even Ryoki himself may not have noticed how alone he is...

"So you wanna know the name of the hotel?"

Aka-chin leaned in even closer.

"Are you really sure you're okay breaking up with him like this? He's never going to come back to the complex, you know."

"Yeah…"

I nodded.

"So it seems you really have moved on to your next big crush!"

"Huh?"

She poked me in the arm.

"To Shinogu!"

"It's…it's nothing like that…yet."

"Yet?" She laughed mischievously.

I blushed so red I couldn't speak and waved my hands frantically.

Without an ounce of regard for the state I was in, Aka-chin just kept going. *Not so loud, Aka-chin!*

"Yes! Yes! Compared to Ryoki, Shinogu's much better! There's nothing to wait for, Hatsumi, so why don't you two get it on!"

"Aka-chin, you move way too fast…"

"Come on, Hatsumi! Love is perishable! If you don't eat it while it's ripe, it'll go bad!"

"I…I know, but…"

"*Puh-leez*, you're giving me a headache! From now on, I'm teaching you the rules of love!"

Aka-chin launched into a sermon that lasted until Mom

shouted at us through the door.

"Girls! Quiet down!"

Sigh. Never a dull moment...

7 At This Rate, You Two Will Never Be Happy

Two days later Shinogu called my cell phone.

"Shinogu, how are you? Are you eating okay? You haven't caught a cold, have you?"

It felt as if I hadn't heard his voice for a long time, so I just kept rattling on.

"What's with you? You sound like we haven't seen each other in years!"

I could hear him laughing at the other end of the line.

"Anyway," he went on, "they're short of hands at that café where you worked before, and I was wondering if you could help us out again."

"I'll do it. I'll definitely do it. Asahi stayed on, right? I've had so much spare time, this'll be perfect!"

"Oh, you're leaving too, Hatsumi?"

Aka-chin was also getting ready to go out.

"Yep. I gotta go to work at that café where I helped out before."

"Mm-hmm...Shinogu works there too, right?"

I coughed.

"What about you?"

"Me? Do I even need to tell you?" She giggled.

Aka-chin took my hand and we dashed out the door.

"You'll be going to the same high school," I said. "You don't need to see each other every day."

"Yeah, but I'm counting on having my first real sex before spring break is over!"

Oh, I get it. Sleeping with Subaru would be her real first time. With someone she really cares about, anyway.

I laughed in understanding. Yeah...good luck, Aka-chin.

Subaru and Asahi waved to us as we ran into the complex's central courtyard.

Subaru blushed when he saw me.

"Subaru...what are you blushing at Hatsumi for?"

Aka-chin looked about ready to blow, but Asahi just laughed.

"Now, now, Akane, this is the first time for Subaru to see Hatsumi as his girlfriend's sister, so he's just a little nervous. Isn't that right, Suba?"

Aka-chin's expression softened when she saw Subaru turn even redder and look away. Asahi had guessed correctly.

"Hey, look over there!"

Asahi pointed to where a bunch of the complex's housewives had gathered.

It was the same sight as always, but the person in the center was different.

After Mrs. Tachibana left, her position had been taken over by a Mrs. Honda, but she didn't have nearly the impact or presence of her predecessor.

"Mrs. Honda seems nice, so maybe from now on this place will be a little more peaceful," Asahi said.

"Yeah, so much happened between the Naritas and Tachibanas."

"Yeah…"

A lot had happened.

It was one incident after the next, so I was always in a panic.

What should I do…? Why is God so cruel?

I was always wondering about stuff like that.

But, for the moment at least, we were at peace.

I felt a bit lonely and sad, though… Had I made the right choice?

"By the way, has anyone seen Azusa lately?"

My friends shook their heads at Akane's question.

"I wonder if he's getting along well with his new family now that his father's remarried," I muttered.

"Yikes! We don't have much time, Hatsumi-chi! We gotta go!"

At Asahi's urging, we parted in pairs to the left and right.

*

"What's up? Long time no see!"

Shinogu's roommate and part-time workmate, Kazama, came up to me as soon as I walked into the café.

"It's great to work with a high school cutie such as yourself again!" he said. "But no dishes this time. You're helping us on the floor. You've been promoted."

He handed me a uniform.

Jeez. I was, like, *totally* freaking out.

"If you have any questions, ask Asahi-chan or Shinogu."

Asahi, who had already put on her uniform, was waving to me from out among the tables.

Was I going to be okay?

"Three coffees, two café-au-laits, and one iced cocoa, please."

"Got it. Two black teas, one latté, and one spaghetti carbonara."

"Huh? What's wrong with this waitress? I wanna talk to the manager! Where's the manager?"

"May I help you?"

Shinogu was beside me in a heartbeat.

"Let me pour you some water…"

"Excuse me!"

"Yes?"

I turned my head.

"You gonna take our order anytime soon?"

"Yes. Just a moment, please."

"Gaaaaah!!!"

I turned around when the customer in front of me yelled. The whole table was soaking wet.

Shinogu ran over with a towel.

"We're really sorry. Are your clothes okay?"

"Excuse me!"

"Yes?"

"Here! Over here!"

"Yes! In a minute!"

While I had been bustling back and forth, a banana peel from a parfait had fallen from my tray onto the floor.

And now it's...oh no...beneath my feeeeeeeeeet!

Yipes! Sliiiiip!

Th-thump!

Craaaash!!!

I was on the verge of careening into a nearby customer when Shinogu slid in to the rescue...and just in time!

"I-I am so sorry!"

"Shinogu, I'm so sorry. I caused you nothing but trouble today. I bet they'll fire me."

I was apologizing in a fit of misery.

"Everyone makes mistakes on their first day. Don't worry. You were actually quite popular. The customers were saying how cute you were."

"Really? You sure?"

"So don't worry about it. Just do your best."

"Okay."

As Shinogu had predicted, I got used to working the floor a little more each day, and before long I was having fun.

But perhaps I should give all the credit to Shinogu, who led me by the hand and taught me everything and made it all so easy to understand.

"Thanks. I enjoyed the meal."

"The food was great."

When customers left the café saying things like that, it really made me happy.

"Good job today."

When we were all done cleaning up, Kazama drove me and Asahi to the station, and then he and Shinogu drove on to their next job, which was at a club.

For some reason that bummed me out.

If possible, I wanted to go home with Shinogu, but he goes to the apartment in Kunitachi when his night jobs are done.

I hesitated a little when I first got back home, but then made up my mind and sent an e-mail to Azusa's cell phone.

\<Azusa...how ya been? Worried cuz I haven't seen u lately. Let me know if u need anything.\>

A little while later, the phone rang.

"Hatsumi, it's me."

"Azusa! Where are you?"

He laughed.

"I'm home. Why so worried?"

"I thought you might have run away like before and gotten everybody upset."

"I won't ever do that again. There's nowhere else for me to go. I found that out last time."

"Azusa..."

"I decided to leave home...but the right way this time."

"What do you mean the 'right' way?"

"I'm moving into my model agency president's condo, and she's moving into a different one."

"..."

"I need to pay rent, so I guess I'll be modeling again. At least for a while."

"It didn't work out with your new family?"

"Well, they're decent enough people, but I just don't feel that close to them. Didn't I tell you before that there's only one family for me?"

"…"

"My dad understood. It's a brand new start, Hatsumi! Can you be happy for me?"

"Of course. So when are you leaving?"

"Tomorrow."

"Tomorrow? Why so suddenly?"

If I hadn't e-mailed him, he would have left without telling me.

Pretty *mean*…

"I already sent all my things."

"Uh-huh…"

"If you wanna come see me off, be at the central entrance of the complex at nine tomorrow morning."

"Okay. I'll tell everyone."

"I only want to see you. I can see everyone else at school."

"Only…me…"

"Yeah. Well, tomorrow then!"

Why only me?

*

"Hey!"

Azusa raised his hands.

He didn't have anything more than a small bag with him.

Maybe because it was Sunday, not many people were outdoors at the complex.

"Thanks for coming to see me off."

"Sure. But I'm still worried."

"Man! You haven't changed a bit. You're always worried about someone other than yourself! You're always worried about me or Shinogu! Did you know how much that always pissed off that four-eyed moron Ryoki?"

Azusa chuckled.

I looked down.

"By the way, whatever happened with you and Shinogu?"

"…"

"He told you he loves you, right?"

I nodded.

"He has that form to annul his adoption by the Naritas all filled in already just so he can go out with you legally any time."

"I…I just don't understand it all very well," I replied.

"What don't you understand?"

"My feelings…or Shinogu's."

"You gotta be kidding! Mr. straight-as-an-arrow

Shinogu has been crazy about you ever since he came to the Naritas, and his feelings wouldn't change so easily!"

"No...but...even though we're working together now, he acts exactly the same way as he did before."

But he did kiss me inside the elevator that once...

And...he held me a couple of times, too.

He even asked me if I could ever love him the way a girl loves a guy...

All these memories were like scenes from a dream.

"He may have already given up on me."

"Oh, please!"

"Ryoki was like that, too. And while I was serious about the breakup, I was still shocked when right after we separated I saw him plastered all over this chick who was pretty, smart, and had big boobs!"

Azusa sighed, and he seemed to be looking around. I was so worked up, though, that I didn't think to ask why.

"You can never be sure someone really loves you," I said timidly.

Azusa shook his head.

"Shinogu probably just wanted to leave you alone while you were unsure of your feelings."

"You really...think so?"

"But, that aside, how do you feel about *him*?"

And that was the crucial question. Point-blank.

"Uh...um..."

I fumbled around for an answer.

The situation had probably reached the state it had because I was unable to respond to Shinogu right away when he confessed his love for me.

If I asked myself now, however, if I could throw myself into his arms, not in desperation, but for real...I didn't think I could.

"But then...I think my feelings are a little different than they were before."

"Really?"

Azusa looked up.

"Yeah. There was this time when I felt as if Shinogu was going to disappear somewhere when he annulled his adoption. Back then I didn't want him to leave because I would miss him...but now if I think about him leaving, I feel like my heart is shriveling up...and it hurts."

"That's a good thing, isn't it?"

Azusa smiled.

"Hatsumi, you and Shinogu are growing closer to each other every day."

"You...you really think so?"

"You're taking it slow, though. Not like with Ryoki."

"But I can't say anything to Shinogu before it's time. I need to be sure of my feelings."

I shook my head.

"Ahhh-ah…"

Azusa stretched his arms over his head and let out a big yawn.

"God dammit! You and Shinogu! Why do you two always think about other people's happiness before your own? At this rate, you two will never be happy! In a way, I guess you are perfect for each other."

He was talking a little louder than was necessary.

"Azusa, is there someone else here?"

I started to look around, but Azusa made me look straight at him.

"Well, I'm taking off," he said. "Let's meet up again sometime, okay? Oh, but I guess we'll see each other at school." He laughed.

Then he turned and walked away, raising one arm in farewell.

"Thanks, Azusa."

He raised his other arm in response.

A while ago, Azusa hurt me really bad.

When he heard from a detective that my father had

been having an affair with his mother, he chose me as the thing my father held most dear. He became my boyfriend to put me off my guard, and then he sicced his friends on me…

But even after all that I still saw him as a friend. When I thought of his sadness and isolation, I just couldn't make myself hate him.

A long time ago…he gave me flowers for my birthday.

I didn't want to lose my precious childhood buddy.

I waved until he was out of sight, and then I went back to my room.

*

Right afterward Shinogu appeared from behind a nearby elm tree, but I didn't notice.

I had no idea that Azusa had called up Shinogu a few minutes after getting off the phone with me the night before and had arranged for Shinogu to be present that morning to hear my feelings.

Shinogu's feelings hadn't changed a bit…

He was fighting to hold back his desire to have me for his own.

I didn't know he was hiding his feelings for me in order not to cause me any further suffering by moving too fast like before.

I also didn't know the secret determination he had made there that day...

Things can't stay this way...
I need to tell Hatsumi my feelings...

8 I Want to Stand by Shinogu
Forever as a Friend

There's the café...

And the nightclub...

And he sometimes works as a bartender or private tutor.

Including all his temporary jobs, I wonder how many jobs Shinogu has.

"Tour conductor?!"

Everyone in the living room was surprised.

"Yeah. They pay pretty well."

"But don't you need some kind of certification to do that?" Aka-chin asked, tilting her head.

"I'm not the main conductor. I'm like an assistant."

"Shinogu, you don't have to work so hard."

Mom sighed. She didn't know that Shinogu had

actually collapsed once from exhaustion.

Shinogu's only response was a slight smile.

He was worried about more than just the money Mom and Dad had spent in feeding him and putting him through school. According to the story Mom had told us a few days earlier, there was also the debt she took up from the man Shinogu's real mother had been living with.

No matter how much Mom insisted Shinogu didn't need to pay back the money, he wouldn't rest until he had repaid it all. He's like that.

"Okay, Hatsumi and Akane, let's go."

Shinogu picked up his bag.

It was the first day of the new school year.

Shinogu was now a sophomore in college.

I was a third-year high school student.

Akane had just entered the same high school as me as a first-year student.

I was in my third year.

I guessed that meant I had to start thinking about the future and whatnot.

"Aka-chin, that's a huge lunch box you got there."

She giggled. "It's part of a new plan. I'm going on my first schoolyard lunch date with Subaru. I'm going to make my lunch every day."

I guessed that meant her plan to clinch it with Subaru during spring break hadn't worked out.

Mom shrugged her shoulders as if wondering how long Akane's latest plan would last.

"I'm outta here, Mom!"

"Akane, it's your turn to take out the trash. Got it?"

It was a usual morning at the Naritas.

In the short time it took Akane to take out the trash, I decided to ask Shinogu a question.

"Shinogu…"

"Yeah?"

I lowered my eyes.

"Oh, nothing."

"What is it? Now you've got me curious."

Shinogu came home sometimes, and when he did he often spent time talking to Mom, and occasionally Dad, about something.

Probably the annulment. I wondered what was going on.

I hoped he'd stay Shinogu Narita at least until he was done with college.

The annulment bugged me so much I couldn't get it out of my head.

But I was too afraid to ask about it…

"Forget it. It's not important."

"Okay, then I'm going on ahead."

All alone, I saw him off.

*

About one week later...

"I'm home!" Shinogu called from the entrance.

Asahi had come over to hang out. We exchanged glances.

"Welcome back!"

We went to greet him, but he wasn't alone.

A young woman was hanging onto his arm like she owned him.

"Hi! I'm in one of Shinogu's seminars. I'm Wakana Nanami."

She was beautiful. Long hair fell in soft curls around her sharply defined features.

She introduced herself in a voice brimming with confidence.

Both Asahi and I swallowed audibly. Before I could stop myself, I glanced at her breasts.

They were...sizeable.

This alone filled me with a sense of inferiority.

"I didn't have any plans for after my job at the café today. She just happened to be there so she came tagging along when I got off."

Shinogu's the kind of person who can't say no.

"Anyway, come on in, Nana."

"…!!"

Did he just call her "Nana"?

Such…intimacy…

She came inside the house with a great show of interest, looking around as if performing an inspection. When she was done she settled down on the sofa.

"This is Hatsumi, the elder of my two sisters."

I nodded.

"She's cute, but she doesn't look like you at all, Shinogu!"

Wham! She hit me right where it hurts.

"And this here is Hatsumi's friend Asahi. She lives in the complex."

"Is that so? But it's not our first time to meet, you know."

At Wakana's words, Asahi nodded uncomfortably. She looked half sick.

"You know how I kept working at the café even after spring break was over? She came in a couple times while I was there."

I guess Wakana would stand out. Even if Asahi wasn't the one who took her order.

"Dad lives away from home for work, Mom's at her part-time job, and my other sister is probably out on a date. My little brother is in the complex's nursery. That about says it for my family."

Shinogu went into the kitchen to get us something to drink.

The three of us were stuck with each other on the sofa.

"So, Hatsumi, all you need is an older sister."

"Uh…yeah. I guess you could say that."

Wakana wore a smile as pure and white as a lace handkerchief.

"You can think of me as your older sister if you want," she said.

"Um…"

"If you do, then I'll be able to come visit again!"

Asahi poked me in the side.

She was shaking her head.

"What?" I whispered, but Wakana interrupted before Asahi could reply.

"What's your name, again?" Wakana asked. "Oh, right! Asahi!"

Wakana lowered her voice and leaned forward.

"I think I should let you know that you'll never make it with Shinogu."

Asahi gasped. Wakana had seen through to her feelings perfectly in only two visits to the café.

"See, there are at least three Shinogu Narita fan clubs at the university. There's even a tour of Shinogu Narita's part-time jobs. Since he doesn't show any interest in girls, though, there was a time when a rumor spread about him not going that way."

At least I knew that "gay" did not apply to Shinogu.

"He plays so hard to get that it's become a matter of womanly pride to get my hands on him."

Wakana was getting worked up.

"Lucky for me he agreed to the tour conductor job. I'm gonna go all out."

And just like that, right there in front of Asahi and me, she bluntly declared her intention to make Shinogu her own.

"Root for me, okay?"

"Sorry to have kept you waiting. Careful, they're hot."

Shinogu came back with four of his special hot orange drinks.

"Wow! These are good," Asahi said.

I nodded in agreement.

Shinogu made them for us at the café sometimes.

Looking a little bored, Wakana dumped hers down her throat in one shot.

"Owowowow! Hot! Hot!"

"I told you it was!"

Just then, Shinogu's cell phone rang.

"Yeah…okay…I got it."

After hanging up, Shinogu rose to his feet.

"Someone called in sick at my bartending job. I gotta go in right away."

"I'll go, too! We can walk to the station together."

Wakana was on her feet in a flash. She wasn't going to let the slightest opportunity slip through her clutches.

*

Asahi shook me by the shoulders.

"The nerve! It doesn't bother you that she might start dating Shinogu?"

"…"

"She certainly is pretty, and she may not be such a bad

person. But...the one he's really in love with is..."

I felt something stir within my heart.

I was shocked when I heard from Kazama that Asahi had fallen in love with Shinogu. Even that Wakana girl had figured it out in no time at all.

Why am I so slow?

"Asahi...I didn't know. I'm so sorry."

"What are you talking about?"

"It must've been terribly hard for you..."

"I'm all right."

"How can that be?"

"It's not such a bad thing to see the one you love be happy."

"Asahi..."

Asahi smiled and blushed.

"You probably already know, but let me tell you everything myself."

She took me by the hand and led me outside.

"I..." And then Asahi continued:

"I have been hopelessly in love with Shinogu ever since you guys moved here. But perhaps I should say 'worship' rather than 'love.' I mean, he's sweet and good-looking and...just plain perfect!

"He was always the most popular boy with all the girls in his class.

"My brother got all the good looks in my family, so I ended up the ugly one. I'm nothing special at all and definitely not good enough for Shinogu.

"Even if I can't be his girlfriend, though, maybe I can be his friend.

"I've helped countless other girls tell him they like him. But he wasn't interested in any of them.

"He probably already has someone he likes.

"That's what I always thought.

"What kind of person could she be? I just had to know.

"But...

"Then I found out that he wasn't your parents' biological child...

"And that the one he has always been in love with was *you*.

"Suddenly everything made sense.

"I don't want to tell him that I'm in love with him *now* and end up making him feel uncomfortable.

"I'm happy the way things are right now. I want to stand by Shinogu forever as a friend."

"Asahi…"

I wiped away my tears.

"That's why I wanted so bad for you to return Shinogu's feelings."

"Yes…I understand…" I said through my sobs.

Shinogu, even way back then, you…

When I thought about that, the pain inside increased.

My heart began beating wildly.

I had never felt like that before.

"I…I'm going to tell Shinogu how I feel…"

"All right!"

Asahi slapped me on the back.

"You go, girl! Knock that college babe outta the way!"

Asahi jumped to her feet.

"*Luuuv* confession! *Luuuv*…confession!"

Asahi—who may have liked Shinogu much more than me—had given me the kick in the pants and the courage I needed.

As I watched her prance around in high spirits, I held my hands before me in two clenched fists and forced back my tears.

9 I Haven't Told Him Yet that He's the One I Love Best and I Won't Let Anyone Take Him Away!

"Hello? Hatsumi?"

A few days later I got a phone call from Wakana.

"How did you get this…"

"I got it from Shinogu."

What was he *thinking*?

"And you might not have heard it from Shinogu yet, but tomorrow we start a tour of famous mountains in Shinshu. Three days, two nights."

"Three days and…two nights?"

"Yep. Shinogu and I will both be working on it. It's the perfect opportunity, don't you think? I've made up my mind to tell him how I feel sometime during the tour."

"…"

"And as his sister, you can help me."

"…"

"Hello? Are you still there?"

"Yeah… You said 'help.' What is it you want me to do?"

"Um…I'm sure you've already guessed. Tell him how sweet I am…say you like me a lot…say all kinds of good things about me! Say how happy you'd be if I were your sister. You know, things like that."

"Oh…kay…"

"But, to tell the truth," she said with a laugh, "it's pretty much a done deal."

"…!"

Wakana could barely contain her elation.

I took a deep breath.

"I mean, he asked me what it is a girl wants more than anything else. I think he's gonna give me a present!"

"Oh…?"

"The last day of the tour is my birthday!"

Suddenly it hit me.

I counted on my fingers.

Yep.

That day was also *my* birthday…

"But just to be sure, don't forget the sister strategy, okay?"

Beep beep beep beep beep beep.

I listened to that sound with my cell phone pressed to my ear long after she had hung up.

Shinogu was coming back home that day. He needed to pick up some stuff for the tour.

All this just when I had been thinking about telling him how *I* felt!

I had been going to talk to him as soon as he got back.

But…he was going to give *her* a present…

Worse still…he was going to do it on *my* birthday…

Shinogu had given me a present every year for my birthday, and he'd always asked me ahead of time what I wanted.

Just the way he'd asked Wakana this time.

"I'm home!"

Shinogu's voice sounded from the entrance.

I couldn't make myself go to greet him.

*

"I gotta work tours for viewing cherry blossoms three days in a row."

"Oh, really?"

Shinogu lied to us over dinner that night.

Shinogu…

"Hey, do you tour conductors ever get romantic with each other or the guests on overnight trips?"

My heart almost jumped out of my chest when Aka-chin asked Shinogu this question.

"No. Besides, I only work day trips."

"Oh."

Aka-chin appeared to lose interest.

"Anyway, you be careful," Mom said. "And cut back on the jobs. The money can wait."

Shinogu nodded.

"Hatsumi, hurry up and eat. Shinogu, can you play with Hii-kun?"

It was the usual Narita dinner-table scene.

Except Shinogu didn't say a single thing to me.

Early the next morning I saw Shinogu off by myself as he was leaving with his mountain-climbing gear.

What do you want for your birthday?

I had waited until the last moment to hear him ask me this question.

"Well, I'm taking off."

He put his hand on the doorknob.

"When I finish with the job I'm coming back here— not to the apartment."

"You didn't have to lie about the cherry-blossom tours," I said.

"Hatsumi…"

"Did you think everyone would worry if you said you were going to stay overnight on a mountain-climbing tour?"

Shinogu sighed.

"No…it…it wasn't that…"

"Was it…because you're going with Wakana?"

"Hatsumi…"

I couldn't bear to look at him.

"Wakana's pretty and she's…a good person. I wouldn't mind having a…a sister like that…"

What was I saying?

Dumb! Majorly dumb! Majorly *majorly* dumb!

I turned my back on a stunned Shinogu and ran to my room.

Bam!

The sound of the front door slamming rang hollowly throughout the house.

Even though it was Golden Week, I didn't feel like going anywhere, so I just stared at the walls all day.

At night my frustration built up.

Maybe by now they'd finished eating dinner and were taking a walk and watching the beautiful starry night sky together...

"Urrrgggh!"

I scratched my head.

While I was taking my sweet ol' time, Shinogu had been snatched up by someone else.

Aka-chin had lectured me about this once.

"Hatsumi, you don't do anything. Whenever you're invited on a date, you just go...and then let it drop. You're always so passive. I've never seen you take action yourself. It would be unfair if you got what you wanted like that! Me, I bust my butt to get who I want!"

She was absolutely right.

I was a coward.

I was *pitiful*...

Come to think of it, a while back when she was trying to get Ryoki, Aka-chin *did* pull a lot of stunts—like falling down on purpose and acting as if her ankle were sprained—all designed to draw him in close to her body.

What's more, at the university there must have been hordes of girls just as elegant and beautiful as Wakana.

I had never thought of that before.

But it must have been true.

I bet it was like that at his workplaces as well.

What if some student he taught privately was a really cute junior-high student like Akane?

What could I do?

He was with them behind closed doors...

Or at clubs full of hypersexy young ladies gushing with pheromones.

I was roadkill…

I stood no chance against them.

*

Poof!

A little devil appeared inside my head. A devilish Hatsumi.

"So are you finally feeling the heat?" she said.

"Don't be ridiculous!" This from a new arrival. An angel Hatsumi.

"What with his cool demeanor of late and other girls popping into the picture," the devil continued, "I'd say you are *way* stressing it."

The angel Hatsumi stewed in silence.

"Don't forget. Shinogu *is* a guy."

The angel spluttered and at last was able to offer a reply.

"I'll tell him how I feel…in a little while."

"In a little while?! Content to drag our ass, are we?"

"…"

"The worst could happen any minute! Quit standing around gaping, you freaking slowpoke!"

"Slowpoke…"

"Come on, let's get the hell outta here!"

"Wha—?"

The little devil laid hold of the angel and they both disappeared.

*

"Good morning…"

"Oh, Hatsumi! You're up early!"

"Yeah…"

I hadn't slept a wink.

"Morning."

Akane was also up. She was going on a hiking date with Subaru.

"Breakfast is ready. Go ahead and eat," Mom said. "And here, this is for you."

Mom placed a big package in front of Akane.

"I packed you lunch."

"Mom! You're the greatest!"

Akane was in the best of spirits. She pressed the lunch box to her cheek.

That was when it happened.

The phone rang.

Mom answered.

"Hello?...Yes, this is the Naritas..."

"Yes...uh-huh...oh..."

From the sound of her voice, something was clearly wrong.

Her hands were trembling.

After hanging up, she slumped to the floor.

"That was Shinogu's friend, Kazama. He said Shinogu went looking for a tourist who got lost in the mountains... and now Shinogu's missing, too..."

"What?" Akane cried.

I couldn't say a word.

My throat was closing up.

"That can't be! He said he was going cherry-blossom viewing..."

I was finally able to make myself speak—

"Actually...he was going mountain-climbing..."

"I guess...he didn't want to worry us."

Mom started chewing her lip.

For a while, I just sat in a daze.

Shinogu was missing...in the mountains...

He might...never...come back?

I might never see him again?

And I had been so rotten to him the last time we talked...

Akane and Subaru canceled their date.

Subaru came over with Asahi.

Dad was taking the bullet train back from Osaka.

Mom buried her face in her hands and cried and cried.

"I told him over and over that he didn't have to worry about the money..."

Everyone was scattered around the room with their heads down.

Asahi sat down beside me.

"Hatsumi, are you all right?"

I came back to myself with a start and took out my cell phone.

"I...I'm going to try calling him! Maybe then..."

The room was silent. Shinogu's phone didn't respond at all.

"Hello? Hello? Shinogu! Answer me! Please!"

"Hatsumi, Shinogu's lost..."

Akane's voice was an almost inaudible whisper.

Dad arrived around lunchtime.

There was still no call from the tour site...

Time passed quietly and slowly.

What was Shinogu doing?

Was he injured?

Was he cold?

Was he scared?

It was almost nightfall.

What if he were attacked by bears or wolves...

"N-no...that can't...happen..."

My mind had started to drift away...

"Hatsumi! Be strong!"

When I came to, I found Subaru had caught me as I toppled off the sofa.

"Subaru...I'm sorry. I just don't know what to do..."

On a usual day Akane would have been on my case asking what the hell I was doing, but that day she just looked worried.

"I know it's difficult," Subaru said, "but let's just wait until he calls. Okay?"

"Hello? May I come in?"

Kazama appeared. He was holding a big plastic bag. It looked like food.

"Hello, everyone. You may all be tired, but you have to eat something to stay strong!"

"Thank you…" Mom said.

"They looked for him all day today…helicopters, the police, firefighters… They conducted a search of the mountain with about a hundred people, but they couldn't find him."

Silence settled over the room.

"They're planning on starting again first thing tomorrow morning."

"Ok. Thank you for everything."

Dad bowed in gratitude.

"Shinogu will be all right. He's a real tough guy."

A convulsive cry escaped me.

"Nnghn…Shinogu…"

I thought I was going insane.

"I'm sorry, Asahi, but could you help Hatsumi to her room for some rest?"

Mom sounded so tired.

"Sure."

Asahi led me to my room and I lay down on my bed.

For the longest time I just let Asahi rub my back.

*

Toward morning I was dozing off when I had a dream.

I was walking through a gauzy mist.

I didn't have much confidence, but I was going in the direction I wanted.

When I turned around, Shinogu was there.

Relieved, I kept going.

Every now and then I would turn around…

And Shinogu was always there.

It was going to be all right.

Shinogu had always protected me.

But still I was anxious every time I turned around…

Worried that he might not be there.

Yes…

If we could just walk along together…

Holding hands so we never got separated...

That way, I'd never have to worry again.

I turned around again as this last thought went through my mind…

But Shinogu was gone.

He was walking away down a side street.

"Shinogu! Don't go! Stay with me!"

No sooner had these words escaped my mouth than he was enshrouded in mist and disappeared.

"Shinogu!"

I awoke with a start.

Asahi was asleep facedown on the bed.

I let her sleep and went into the living room.

"Hatsumi..."

No one looked like they'd gotten much sleep.

"Hatsumi, today's search is going to start soon. Let's keep our hopes high," Kazama said.

I nodded.

"Yeah..."

As Kazama had said, Shinogu was going to be all right.

I tried to have courage.

If everything had really been all right, though, Shinogu would have been home already.

When I thought about that, my inner unrest started all over again.

"Hatsumi, eat something," Mom said. "Here's the food Kazama and Subaru brought."

I shook my head.

I sat on the edge of the sofa and hugged my knees.

I'd never experienced such anxiety before.

The afternoon passed…and still no news.

Kazama called the tour site periodically, but there were no developments.

To make matters worse, rain had started to fall and the search was running into difficulties.

The clock struck two, then four…then six.

It was almost nightfall.

"Another day is ending. Poor Shinogu… What if he's dead?"

Aka-chin was mumbling, her expression blank.

"Akane!" Mother scolded.

Shinogu…dead…

Shinogu's…dead…

I stood up.

"I'll go look for him!"

Kazama stopped me as I darted for the door.

He pulled me into Shinogu's room.

"Hatsumi, you've gotta calm down. I'm sure Shinogu's all right."

"But...they've been searching for two days already..."

"Hatsumi, this is for you..."

Kazama pulled a small package from his pocket and handed it to me.

"It's a gift from Shinogu."

"Gift?"

"Today's your birthday, right? Shinogu ordered it, but it got delivered to the apartment so I brought it with me."

My mind went blank.

"But isn't it for Wakana?"

"As if! Shinogu only ever thinks about you. He forced this job as a tour conductor on himself just so he could buy you this."

"..."

"Look. Shinogu's so googly-eyed over you he'd take vows and become a monk if anyone else ever got you!"

"Are you sure? Then why..."

Shinogu asked Wakana what it is a girl wants more than anything else. *That was for me?*

"What should I do?"

Tears dropped from my eyes.

To think I doubted Shinogu for even a moment.

I was so ashamed of myself.

I was *wretched.*

Shinogu…

I wondered what he was doing at that moment.

Was he okay?

Was he hurt?

Or was he…

What would I do if…if I really never had the chance to see him again…

"I haven't told him yet…that I love him…even though I still can't say what type of love it is," I cried, pressing the little box to my chest.

"I haven't told him yet that he's the one I love best and I won't let anyone take him away!"

Kazama's cell phone rang.

"Hello?"

Kazama listened to the caller for a while and then let out an exclamation.

"Thank God!"

At the same time he pumped a fist high into the air.

10 If You Don't Mind Being with Me, Would You Wear That?

Kazama was driving me to the hospital in Nagano where Shinogu had been hospitalized.

"It's just like him to go looking for one of the tourists even though he was just a part-timer."

"Yeah. But I'm glad the tourist was okay."

"Too bad Shinogu got hurt instead."

"I wonder what his condition is."

"Well, we won't know until we get there. But really, I'm glad they found him."

I nodded.

*

"Hey everyone, Shinogu and the tourist were found

and taken to safety!"

When everyone had heard Kazama's news, they'd been overcome with relief. The very next moment, however, they sent up a roar of cheers.

Shinogu...

I fully realized that day how much Shinogu had become a member of our family.

"I'm going to go see him."

"Yes, you do that," Mom had said with a smile that lit up her whole face.

"But before that, Hatsumi...Happy Birthday!"

Mom produced a cake from the fridge.

"We all want to congratulate you before you go."

"Mom...thank you."

I felt like crying again.

I once overheard a conversation between Mom and Shinogu.

It was clear Mom already knew the way Shinogu felt about me.

She said it would be nice if things worked out between me and him, because then, even if he officially left the family, he wouldn't really be leaving, and both of us would always be her children.

It probably wouldn't happen until way in the future,

but I thought it would be great if I could see Mom smile for this very reason.

*

"So what was the present?" Kazama asked.

"I haven't opened it yet," I replied. "I wanted to open it with Shinogu...so..."

"Ohhh, I see..."

The car rapidly approached its destination.

"By the way, how're things between Akane and that baby-faced boyfriend of hers?"

"What do you mean?"'

Hold on a minute... Why was Kazama asking this?

Sensing my suspicion, Kazama flashed a grin.

"Hey, I'll give it to you straight. I want Akane for myself. Adorable little Subaru is all right, but don't you think Akane and I would make a better couple?"

Hmmmm... He said it so simply in that cool style of his that I couldn't bring myself to say anything in response.

"I...had no idea..."

Subaru...hang in there!

*

Without realizing it, I nodded off from exhaustion.

"Hatsumi. We're there."

I jerked awake.

Before my eyes was a cozy, clean-looking little hospital.

We asked for Shinogu's room at the nurses' center.

"Um…how're his injuries?" I asked one of the nurses.

"He has a minor fracture in his right leg. He'll be able to leave the hospital in about two weeks."

Kazama and I each heaved a sigh of relief.

Cautiously, I peeked into Shinogu's hospital room.

He was asleep.

Wakana was seated at his bedside.

She stood up when we entered.

"I heard you've been keeping him company since they found him…" Kazama said. "Thanks."

"It means a lot," I said, bowing my head. "Really."

Wakana looked exhausted and even had circles under her eyes. She smiled faintly.

"It was nothing… I guess I'll be going now…"

She quietly made her way toward the door.

Partway there she turned around and looked at me.

"It seems like Shinogu's special someone was a girl with the same birthday as me..."

I stood over Shinogu.

He must've been so tired.

He must have had a really difficult time.

I'm sorry...

I couldn't protect you.

My heart ached all over again.

My eyes kept filling with tears as I sat on one of the stools by his bed and watched his face while he slept.

He had said that happiness would run out if you didn't save up.

If I stayed beside him forever, then maybe his happiness would never run out...

Because I'd be happy and he'd be happy and we'd have two whole persons' worth of happiness.

I felt this way because just being there beside him made me ever so...ever so...happy.

"Ha...tsumi..."

Shinogu opened his eyes.

"You came..."

I nodded.

I glanced to one side. Kazama had chosen that moment to disappear.

"I'm so sorry I…made you worry."

I shook my head repeatedly.

Tears fell left and right.

I took the small package from my bag.

"Thank you for this."

Shinogu smiled weakly.

"Kazama?"

I nodded.

"I actually had some suspicions about you and Wakana. Sorry."

Shinogu looked at me in surprise.

"Come to think of it, Nana did say today was her birthday. When I said 'Happy Birthday' she started crying… Did I do something wrong?"

"Yeah…I guess you did. A little."

Now maybe Wakana would give up on Shinogu once and for all.

"May I open it?"

"Go ahead."

When I opened the package, I gasped in surprise.

"A ring!"

It was small, but it had a diamond.

I stared at it with wide eyes for a while.

"If it's a bother, you can just throw it away. But if you wouldn't mind, could you just hold on to it? All I ask is you hold on to it."

"Shinogu…"

"I just wanted to express my feelings to you clearly," Shinogu continued.

"I was thinking about submitting the annulment form once I saved up enough money to repay our parents even a little for raising me—even if just the school expenses— but now I also want to repay the debt that Mom mentioned the other day. It's shameful, I know, but it'll take some time to do that. When that day comes, though, if…you don't mind being with me…would you wear that?

My heart felt ready to explode. All of this somehow hurt…

But I was overjoyed.

I couldn't say anything at all.

All I could do was slowly nod.

Shinogu seemed to be smiling.

I had so many things I wanted to say…

But my heart was so full of emotion that I couldn't say a word.

"This…isn't a dream, is it?" Shinogu asked.

I shook my head and wiped away my tears.

Yes...

He had said something similar once before, the time he'd watched over me from inside a nearby car one cold night. Shinogu said he was going to work, but he actually stuck around to make sure I was alright.

"May I hold you?" he had asked.

I had thought I needed to help *him* get warm...

...so I nodded.

Thump...thump... thump...

With our bodies clasped together, I could feel his heartbeat.

In the end I was the one who was warmed by *him*.

When Shinogu let me go, he said, "I can't believe...I was holding you like that... I felt like if I let go you might vanish...or that maybe I was just dreaming..."

And I had said, "It's not a dream."

God, I'm really sorry.

I...I love my own sister.

I promise to not tell anyone. To keep it a secret.

So...

...please, God...

Let Hatsumi always be by my side.

Please, let Hatsumi be mine alone.

Shinogu had always felt this way…
He was looking at me and smiling slightly.

*

"Brudder!"

"Shut up! I'm not your brother. I'm leaving your house. So stop calling me that!"

"Waaah…"

"Stop it. I said, stop it! Your mommy'll find us. I'm going home. Even if I'm all alone there. I'm going home…by myself… So there…"

"Doan cry, Brudder. Do you have a owie? Doan cry. Gubboy, gubboy.

"Iss okay. Owie go 'way. Hami-tan make owie go way. You be okay. So doan go, pleez? Hami-tan love my brudder. Love my brudder."

"Go home, will you…I told you to stop following me around…"

"No! Hami-tan stay with my brudder."

"I'm not your brother… Achoo!"

"You cold?"

"Leave me alone."

"Hami-tan make you warm."

"Why're you rubbing me like that?"

"Get warm." She sniffed, then sneezed.

"Hey! You're the one who's cold."

"Hami-tan not cold. Hami-tan with my brudder so not cold!"

I'll be with brudder.
Get warm.

*

I lied when I had said I forgot inside the elevator.

That was the first time I knew what it meant to feel warm...

"Hatsumi. Happy eighteenth birthday."

"Thank you..."

Shinogu lightly closed his eyes.

He fell back asleep, and I held his hand gently in my own.

"It's so *warm*."

I held the ring tightly against my chest.

I'm sure...some time soon...

Yes...it won't be long...

Whether he finishes repaying his debt or not...

I'll stop viewing him as my brother.

I'm certain of it.

My feelings will grow to suit this ring.

I just know it.

The next time Shinogu wakes up...

I'm going to lay my heart bare...

I close my eyes, still holding his hand tightly in my own.

I see Shinogu in my mind, but this time, rather than watching out for me from behind, I can see him walking with me side by side.

I can clearly see the two of us...

...together.

The End

Afterword

Whether you're a fan of the manga or are reading *Hot Gimmick* for the first time, hello!

My name is Megumi Nishizaki, and I'm the one who wrote this special version of *HG*.

It is always nerve-wracking to novelize a manga series as popular as this one.

"You ruined the way I imagined it!"

"I hate it!"

"I'll kick your @$$!"

...etc.

I'm such a coward that for a few days after the publishing date I was cringing in my closet from fear that someone who didn't like what I had written would break into my place and harass me.

HG depicts the youthful psychology of its characters with immense sensitivity, but since I'm not as young as I used to be, it wasn't easy for me to do this... (Boo-hoo...)

Well, anyway, the ending of this novel is slightly different from the original story.

In the manga, Hatsumi and Ryoki end up happily together (Arrgggh!)...but then what happened to Shinogu? Was he really going to lock himself away forever in some monastery? Certainly not!

So...

I wrote a story based on the idea of what would happen if Hatsumi hadn't met Ryoki at his secret place at the very end of the original story!

Yes, all you Shinogu fans around the world, here is what you've been waiting for!

First of all, you're able to find out in depth about Shinogu's childhood.

And what's more, this is a story in which it seems very probable that Hatsumi and Shinogu will become a couple!!!

"What?"

"Don't beat around the bush!"

"What do you mean?"

If you feel this way, it'll all make sense once you've read this book.

So come on now and move your body over to the cashier!

Even if you're a fan of Ryoki's, why not read it just for fun? (Heh.)

Azusa's in it a lot, too, so you Azusa fans should read it, too!

Miki Aihara began helping me way back at the stage of drafting the story line. Thank you so much for your help and for your great illustrations, Miki! I am also very much indebted to my publisher, O-sama.

And finally I'd like to offer my thanks to all you readers who are now connected to me through this book! Thank you so very much!

I look forward to meeting you again someday!

This has been a message from Megumi Nishizaki—who recently crashed for a grand total of nineteen straight hours of sleep!

Hello! This is Miki Aihara.

How was *Hot Gimmick S* (the "Shinogu Ending" version)? I would have loved to write and illustrate it as a manga if I could have.

Because I'm a gamer, I'm not averse to the idea of a story having different endings depending on the choices the characters make along the way. I actually like the idea that in so doing it is possible to look at the same story from a number of different angles. For this reason we decided on publishing this novel.

In the original manga, Hatsumi chose Ryoki, but what if she had chosen Shinogu? It would be great if readers could enjoy this story as an alternate ending following on the heels of volume 11 of the manga.

This type of attempt is actually quite rare. I'm pretty nervous about what each reader's reaction will be, but I'll be ecstatic if people enjoy it.
Ryoki fans could just ignore this as a parallel story…while Shinogu fans can regard this as having the true ending.

Finally, I would like to express my sincerest appreciation to Megumi Nishizaki, who made a great novel out of my convoluted story line.
Thank you so very much.

Miki Aihara
October 2005

Miki Aihara

A Gemini born on June 10 in Shizuoka Prefecture. Her blood type is A. She made her debut in 1991 with *Lip Conscious!*, published in *Bessatsu Shojo Comic*. Her hobbies are watching various kinds of movies and shopping for clothes. Currently she is a major contributor to *Betsucomi*. Her published manga include *Hot Gimmick*, *Sensei no Okiniiri* (Teacher's Pet), *Seiten Taisei* (The Clear, Wide Blue Sky), *So Bad!*, *Tokyo Boys & Girls* (also available from VIZ Media) and *Sora ni Taiyou ga Aru Kagiri* (As Long as There Is a Sun in the Sky), among others.

Megumi Nishizaki

A Pisces born on February 29 with blood type O. Because of her ultra fickle personality (or perhaps because of a lack of talent?), she is someone who moves from job to job and lives a free and easy life. She rarely gets passionate about anything and is easily bored. She does, however, have a romantic side ♥. She's a free spirit deeply in love with the simple life. For Palette Bunko she has written such books as the *Shishunki Miman Okotowari* (No Pre-Teens Allowed) novels, *Fushigi Yûgi Gaiden*, and the *Ceres Celestial Legend* episode series, among others.

Thank you for reading Hot Gimmick S.
Now please turn to the last page to
discover an unforgottable scene
about Hatsumi & Shinogu.

Now please turn to the last page to

HAMI-CHAN WITH MY BRUDDER, NOT COLD!

HAMI-CHAN NOT COLD.

SQUEAK

SQUEAK

HAMI-CHAN MAKE...

〈SNIF〉

HEY! YOU'RE THE ONE WHO'S COLD.

AH-CHOO!

Next to each other.

Me and Shinogu.

Keeping...

warm...

STOP FOLLOWING ME!

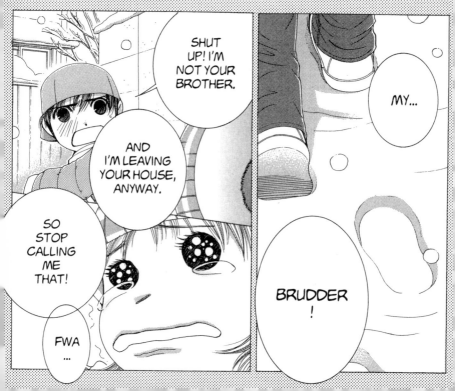

SHUT UP! I'M NOT YOUR BROTHER.

AND I'M LEAVING YOUR HOUSE, ANYWAY.

SO STOP CALLING ME THAT!

FWA...

MY...

BRUDDER!

WAS... THE... ...? YEAH... THIN...

DIDN'T SOME- THING LIKE THIS HAPPEN BEFORE ...?

WHEN WE WERE REALLY LITTLE... WE WERE FREEZING, AND...

...WHAT WAS IT?

I DON'T REMEM- BER...

AS LONG AS YOU'RE NEXT TO ME, I'LL BE WARM.

I'LL BE FINE.

HEY!

NO, SHINOGU. KEEP IT. YOU'LL FREEZE.

IT'S ALWAYS BEEN LIKE THAT.

EVER SINCE WE WERE KIDS.

...

EY...

IT...

Hatsumi & Shinogu

**From volume 9
Hot Gimmick.**